Disney

OUT OF THIS WORLD

CARTOON TALES

Disney
OUT OF THIS WORLD
CARTOON TALES

ADAPTED BY SCOTT PETERSON

Disney
PRESS

New York

Artwork for *Lilo & Stitch* by Massimiliano Narciso, Anna Merli, Sonia Matrone, Gabriella Matta, Federico Bertolucci, Dario Calabria
Artwork for *Peter Pan* by Mario Cortes, Yves Chagnaud
Artwork for *Treasure Planet* by Mario Cortes, Massimo Rocca, Andrea Cagol, Dario Calabria

Printed in Singapore
First Edition
1 3 5 7 9 10 8 6 4 2
Library of Congress Catalog Card Number: 2004112384

ISBN 0-7868-3609-1

For more Disney Press fun, visit www.disneybooks.com

CONTENTS

JUMBA JUKIBA, A RENEGADE SCIENTIST, HAD CREATED THE UNIVERSE'S MOST DANGEROUS WEAPON. AND THE GALACTIC FEDERATION, WHICH GOVERNED THIS REGION OF SPACE, WAS *NOT* HAPPY!

HE IS BULLETPROOF, FIREPROOF, AND CAN THINK FASTER THAN A SUPERCOMPUTER.

HIS ONLY INSTINCT IS TO DESTROY EVERYTHING HE TOUCHES.

HE'S A WEAPON.

A LITTLE ONE.

HMM.

PERHAPS IT CAN BE REASONED WITH.

EXPERIMENT 626, GIVE US SOME SIGN THAT YOU UNDERSTAND—

MEEGA, NALA **KWEEESTA!**

HOW **FRESH!**

626'S BAD ATTITUDE GOT HIM LOCKED UP IN A SPECIAL CELL. BUT, OF COURSE, KEEPING THE UNIVERSE'S MOST DANGEROUS WEAPON LOCKED UP IS NO EASY TASK . . .

AHH! HE'S LOOSE! RED ALERT! STOP HIM!

626 JUMPED INTO AN ESCAPE POD AND FLED THE SHIP!

BLAAMM!!

BA-BLAMM!!

MEANWHILE, ON THE BRIDGE . . .

THE ALARM! WHO . . . ?

IT'S 626. HE'S ESCAPED, SIR!

626 LANDED ON A HEAVILY POPULATED PLANET. THE GRAND COUNCILWOMAN KNEW JUST WHAT NEEDED TO BE DONE.

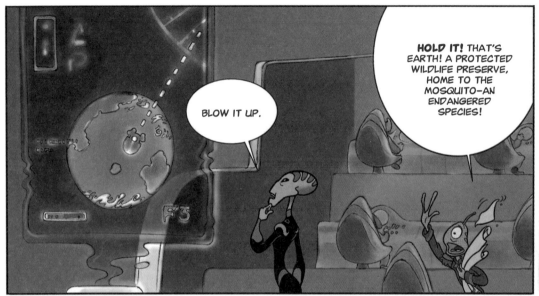

BLOW IT UP.

HOLD IT! THAT'S EARTH! A PROTECTED WILDLIFE PRESERVE, HOME TO THE MOSQUITO–AN ENDANGERED SPECIES!

AND YOU ARE?

AGENT PLEAKLEY. I'VE STUDIED EARTH FOR A VERY LONG TIME AND–

IS THERE ANY OTHER INTELLIGENT LIFE ON THIS . . . "EARTH"?

WELL . . . NO. BUT THE MOSQUITO'S FOOD OF CHOICE ARE THE PRIMITIVE HUMANOIDS THAT HAVE COLONIES ALL OVER THE PLANET.

SO AN EXPERT MUST BE SENT, THEN?

YES! AN EXPERT . . . OH . . . OH . . . UH . . . HEH . . . YOU MEAN ME, HUH?

AGENT PLEAKLEY WAS NOT EXACTLY COMFORTABLE WITH HIS MISSION, BUT HE COULDN'T SAY NO TO THE COUNCILWOMAN. AND, TO MAKE MATTERS WORSE, HE FOUND OUT THAT SHE WOULD BE SENDING JUMBA, TOO! JUMBA— WHO WAS SO ANGRY AT THE PRESS HE'D RECEIVED THAT HE *ATE* THE NEWSPAPER.

SO . . . EXPERIMENT 626—

—IS GONE, YES?

YES HE IS. WE NEED YOU TO BRING HIM BACK.

BUT WITHOUT HURTING THE PLANET HE'S ON!

OH, YES. THAT TOO.

IT'S A VERY DELICATE PLANET!

SO, TELL ME, MY LITTLE ONE-EYED ONE . . .

. . . WHAT IS THE **NAME** OF THIS PLANET?

NOBODY LIKES TO BE CALLED NAMES. AND LILO WAS NO EXCEPTION.

AM NOT!

ARE TOO-EEEEEK!

AM NOT, AM NOT, AM **NOT**!

EVERYBODY! CALM DOWN!

YOU WACKO!

LILO . . .

I'M SORRY. I WON'T DO IT AGAIN.

EVEN AFTER DANCE CLASS, WITH TIME TO CALM DOWN, LILO WAS STILL UPSET.

I CALLED YOUR SISTER. SHE SAID TO WAIT HERE FOR HER.

EVEN THOUGH SHE WAS FEELING DOWN, LILO THOUGHT GIVING HER CLASSMATES ANOTHER TRY MIGHT CHEER HER UP.

ARE YOU GONNA PLAY DOLLS?

YOU DON'T HAVE A DOLL.

SURE I DO! THIS IS SCRUMP.

I MADE HER, BUT HER HEAD'S TOO BIG, SO I PRETEND A BUG LAID EGGS IN HER EARS AND–

GASP!

THE OTHER KIDS RAN AWAY. LILO WAS USED TO NOT FITTING IN, BUT IT DIDN'T MAKE IT ANY EASIER.

SHE PICKED SCRUMP UP AND HEADED HOME, ALONE AND SAD.

LILO?

LILO! WHERE ARE YOU?

HEY! WATCH IT, BOZO-HEAD!

SCREEECH!

LILO? I KNOW YOU'RE THERE.

GO AWAY.

LEAVE ME ALONE.

LILO THOUGHT SHE'D BE ABLE TO KEEP NANI OUT OF THE HOUSE BY NAILING THE DOOR SHUT.

THE BOZO-HEAD ALSO HAPPENED TO BE COBRA BUBBLES—THE *SOCIAL WORKER!* OH, BOY! NANI HAD TOLD LILO EXACTLY HOW TO ANSWER THE SOCIAL WORKER. UNFORTUNATELY, LILO DIDN'T ALWAYS GET INSTRUCTIONS RIGHT!

NANI REALIZED THAT THIS VISIT HAD **NOT** GONE WELL.

THEN LILO SPOTTED SOMETHING OUTSIDE HER WINDOW.

A SHOOTING STAR!

GET OUT! I HAVE TO WISH!

NANI LEFT THE ROOM, BUT PEEKED IN TO HEAR THE WISH LILO WOULD MAKE.

I NEED A FRIEND—SOMEONE WHO WON'T RUN AWAY. PLEASE SEND ME AN ANGEL . . .

OF COURSE, YOU SHOULD ALWAYS BE CAREFUL WHAT YOU WISH FOR . . .

HEE-HE-HE-HE-HEE!!!

. . . SOMETIMES YOU DON'T GET EXACTLY WHAT YOU EXPECTED.

THAT WAS NO SHOOTING STAR LILO HAD SEEN. IT WAS 626 CRASHING TO EARTH. AND HE WAS ABOUT TO FIND THAT THE PLANET WAS *FULL* OF UNEXPECTED THINGS! FOR EXAMPLE, HE HAD NEVER SEEN A FROG BEFORE.

VRRrrr...

THE FROG DISTRACTED HIM SO MUCH THAT HE DIDN'T NOTICE A TRUCK ROUNDING THE CURVE!

SLAM

OF COURSE, 626 COULDN'T BE HURT. AND WHEN THE TRUCK DRIVERS GOT OUT TO SEE WHAT THEY HAD HIT, THEY SAW HIM STANDING THERE.

UH . . . WE'D BETTER CALL SOMEBODY.

AND THAT'S HOW 626 WOUND UP IN A HAWAIIAN DOG POUND! AND GUESS WHO HAD DECIDED TO DROP IN TO THAT POUND THE VERY NEXT DAY . . . ?

HI. MY SISTER WOULD LIKE TO ADOPT A PUPPY.

WELL, SURE— WHY DON'T YOU COME PICK ONE OUT?

HELLO? ARE THERE ANY DOGS HERE WHO WANT A HOME?

ADOPT TODAY

626 CHANGED HIS SHAPE SO THAT HE FIT IN BETTER WITH THE DOGS. THAT'S WHEN LILO FIRST SAW HIM!

HELLO!

HAY . . . LOW.

WOW.

NOT EVERYONE WAS QUITE AS EXCITED AS LILO ABOUT HER NEW-FOUND FRIEND, THOUGH.

NO! ANY DOG BUT THAT ONE!

THAT'S A DOG?!

A BRIEF FIGHT LATER . . .

THAT'S MY DOG.

HIS NAME IS STITCH.

OKAY, IF YOU INSIST . . . THE LICENSE COSTS TWO DOLLARS.

PUPPY

CAN I BORROW TWO DOLLARS?

NANI GAVE LILO THE MONEY, AND THEY WERE ALL SET!

YOU'VE GOT YOURSELF A . . . DOG . . . THING.

ADOPT

626, NOW CALLED STITCH, NOTICED A STRANGE BEAM OUTSIDE THE POUND. HE WALKED OVER, ON ALL FOURS, OF COURSE, TO CHECK IT OUT.

JUMBA AND PLEAKLEY REALIZED THAT THEY WOULD NEED DISGUISES. WHILE THEY PUT ON THEIR COSTUMES, NANI SAID GOOD-BYE TO LILO AND STITCH.

I GOTTA GET TO WORK. STICK AROUND TOWN AND STAY OFF THE ROADS, OKAY?

LOOK! IT'S MY FRIENDS!

SORRY I BIT YOU. AND PULLED YOUR HAIR. AND PUNCHED YOU IN THE FACE.

APOLOGY **NOT** ACCEPTED. NOW GET OUT OF MY WAY.

WHAT'S **THAT**?

MY NEW DOG, STITCH!

EWWW. YUCK! GET IT AWAY FROM ME! I'M GONNA GET A DISEASE.

MEANWHILE, JUMBA AND PLEAKLEY HAD FINALLY CAUGHT UP WITH STITCH! AND THEY WERE . . . UMMM . . . "DISGUISED" SO THAT THEY WOULD FIT IN ON EARTH.

GROWL!

BUT STITCH SPOTTED JUMBA AND PLEAKLEY RIGHT AWAY!

OH GREAT! HE'S ESCAPED.

HIS DESTRUCTIVE PROGRAMMING IS TAKING EFFECT. HE WILL BE DRAWN TO LARGE CITIES WHERE HE WILL BACK UP SEWERS, REVERSE STREET SIGNS, AND STEAL EVERYONE'S LEFT SHOE!

SHORTLY THEREAFTER, LILO AND STITCH ARRIVED AT THE BEACH.

SCREECH!

WHEN THEY GOT TO THE OCEAN, LILO BREATHED IN THE SWEET SALT AIR.

IT SURE IS NICE TO BE ON AN ISLAND WITH NO LARGE CITIES!

UGH!

ARE YOU OKAY?

STITCH HATED WATER, WHICH, HERE ON THE ISLAND, WAS ALL AROUND HIM. AND HE HAD AN INSTINCT TO DESTROY CITIES. THIS PLACE WAS **NOT** GOING TO BE FUN FOR HIM.

BUT THAT NIGHT, LILO TOOK STITCH TO THE RESTAURANT WHERE NANI WORKED. AND THE RESTAURANT WAS FUN NO MATTER WHAT TYPE OF SCENE YOU WERE LOOKING FOR!

HMM?

THIS IS YOU, AND HERE'S YOUR BADNESS LEVEL. IT'S UNUSUALLY HIGH FOR SOMEONE YOUR SIZE.

LILO, YOUR DOG CAN'T SIT AT THE TABLE!

STITCH IS TROUBLED. HE NEEDS DESSERT.

WHILE NANI WENT TO GET DESSERT, HER FRIEND DAVID WALKED OVER TO LILO AND STITCH.

DAVID! I GOT A NEW DOG!

WHOA, YOU SURE IT'S A DOG?

THEN, NANI RETURNED WITH DESSERT.

HI, DAVID.

OH, HI, NANI . . . LISTEN, IF YOU'RE NOT BUSY TOMORROW NIGHT—

DAVID, I'VE TOLD YOU, I - I CAN'T . . .

I'VE GOT A LOT TO DEAL WITH RIGHT NOW.

DON'T WORRY, DAVID— SHE LIKES YOU. I READ HER DIARY.

REALLY?

SNIFF SNIFF

LILO SHOULD HAVE BEEN PAYING AS MUCH ATTENTION TO HER NEW PET AS SHE HAD TO HER BIG SISTER'S DIARY. . .

JUMBA AND PLEAKLEY WERE IN THE RESTAURANT. AND THEY WERE BAITING STITCH!

I'VE **GOT** YOU!

THEN, NANI'S BOSS ARRIVED TO SEE WHAT WAS GOING ON.

34

NANI'S BOSS WAS NOT PLEASED AT ALL. IN FACT, HE WAS **SO** ANGRY THAT HE FIRED NANI! AND BACK AT HOME, NANI HAD A WORD WITH LILO.

THIS THING HAS GOT TO GO!

NO! WE **ADOPTED** HIM!

HE'S **CREEPY**, LILO—I DON'T EVEN THINK HE'S REALLY A **DOG**.

WHAT ABOUT 'OHANA? DAD SAID 'OHANA MEANS FAMILY! AND FAMILY MEANS . . .

GRR . . .

. . . NOBODY GETS LEFT BEHIND. . .

. . . OR FORGOTTEN. I **HATE** WHEN YOU USE 'OHANA AGAINST ME.

IT'S POWERFUL STUFF, THAT 'OHANA.

STITCH WAS HERE FOR GOOD, SO LILO TOOK HIM
UPSTAIRS TO SHOW HIM WHERE HE'D BE SLEEPING.

THIS IS **YOUR** BED, WITH A DOLLY AND A BOTTLE OF COFFEE.

THAT'S SCRUMP—SHE'S RECOVERING FROM SURGERY. HERE—THIS MIGHT MAKE YOU FEEL BETTER.

LILO PUT A LEI AROUND STITCH'S NECK. AND WHAT DO YOU KNOW? IT DID MAKE HIM FEEL BETTER!

BUT NOT FOR LONG . . . HE WAS SOON ANTSY AGAIN. AND HE STARTED BUILDING SOMETHING.

WHAT ARE YOU MAKING?

WOW. SAN FRANCISCO!

IF STITCH COULDN'T FIND A REAL CITY TO DESTROY, HE'D JUST MAKE HIS OWN . . . AND DESTROY **THAT** ONE!

ROWR!

THAT'S IT! NO MORE COFFEE FOR YOU.

JUMBA
AND
PLEAKLEY
WATCHED
FROM
AFAR.

THE LITTLE GIRL IS WASTING HER TIME. 626 CANNOT BE TAUGHT TO IGNORE ITS DESTRUCTIVE PROGRAMMING. ITS NATURE WILL WIN OUT.

LOOK! A MOSQUITO HAS CHOSEN ME AS HER PERCH!

AND ANOTHER ONE! WHY, IT'S A WHOLE FLOCK! THEY'RE NUZZLING ME . . . THEY'RE . . . THEY'RE . . .

OW! THEY'RE **BITING** ME!!!

BACK AT LILO'S HOUSE, IT WAS CLEAR THE LITTLE GIRL WAS NOT GOING TO GIVE UP ON STITCH . . . EVEN IF JUMBA THOUGHT SHE *WAS* WASTING HER TIME.

THIS IS THE STORY OF THE UGLY DUCKLING. HE'S SAD BECAUSE HE'S ALONE AND NO ONE WANTS HIM.

BUT SEE? HE JUST NEEDED TO FIND HIS FAMILY. NOW HE'S HAPPY BECAUSE HE KNOWS WHERE HE BELONGS. THAT'S ALL ANYONE NEEDS.

LILO AND STITCH DIDN'T KNOW IT, BUT THEIR OWN LITTLE FAMILY WAS ABOUT TO GET A SUPRISE THE NEXT MORNING.

AND THAT SUPRISE WASN'T PLEASANT! IT WAS COBRA BUBBLES. AND HE WAS **NOT** HAPPY.

YOU GOT FIRED.

WELL . . . ACTUALLY I **QUIT** THAT JOB BECAUSE, YOU KNOW, THE HOURS WERE NOT CONDUCIVE TO RAISING A CHILD . . .

OW.

WHOA.

STITCH, NO!

THUS FAR YOU HAVE BEEN ADRIFT IN THE SHELTERED HARBOR OF MY PATIENCE, NANI, BUT I CANNOT IGNORE YOUR BEING JOBLESS. AND NEXT TIME, I EXPECT THAT . . . DOG . . . TO BE A MODEL CITIZEN. GOOD-BYE!

STITCH? A *MODEL CITIZEN*? LIKE *THAT* WAS GOING TO HAPPEN. STILL, BILLS HAVE TO BE PAID. SO NANI WENT JOB HUNTING. UNFORTUNATELY, SHE HAD TO BRING LILO AND STITCH ALONG.

WHILE NANI TRIED TO FIND WORK, LILO HAD HER *OWN* WORK CUT OUT FOR HER. SHE NEEDED TO TEACH STITCH HOW TO BECOME A MODEL CITIZEN!

FIRST: DANCING.

NOT NOW, DEAR—I NEED TO HIRE SOMEONE.

I KNOW—THAT'S ME!

WHO'S ME?

WHAT?

HANDS ON YOUR HIPS . . . AND . . .

SCHWOOOOOP!

UNFORTUNATELY, *LILO'S* JOB STARTED TO INTERFERE WITH NANI'S JOB *HUNTING*. SEE, STITCH WASN'T EXACTLY A *GRACEFUL* DANCER.

AND THE SAME THING PRETTY MUCH HAPPENED AT THE *NEXT* FIVE PLACES WHERE NANI APPLIED FOR A JOB. MAYBE SHE SHOULD HAVE LEFT STITCH HOME. IN A CAGE. WITH NO KEY.

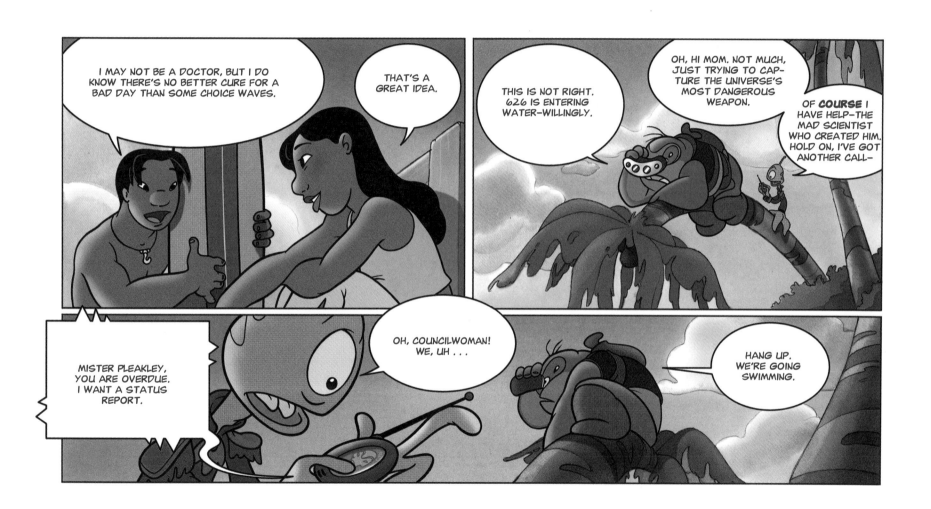

DOWN IN THE WATER, EVERYONE WAS HAVING A GREAT TIME. BUT THINGS WERE ABOUT TO GET *UGLY.*

SWOOOSH!

LILO?

WHERE'S STITCH?

STITCH WAS CAUGHT BY JUMBA AND PULLED UNDER THE WATER! AND WHEN LILO TRIED TO HELP HIM, SHE GOT PULLED UNDER, TOO!

DAVID AND NANI BROUGHT LILO AND STITCH TO THE SHORE. BUT COBRA BUBBLES HAD SEEN EVERYTHING THAT HAD HAPPENED.

I CAN EXPLAIN . . .

I KNOW YOU'RE TRYING, NANI. BUT YOU NEED TO THINK ABOUT WHAT'S BEST FOR LILO. EVEN IF THAT'S NOT **YOU**.

NANI?

I NEED TO TAKE LILO HOME NOW. WE HAVE A LOT TO TALK ABOUT.

YOU KNOW STITCH, I REALLY BELIEVED THEY HAD A CHANCE. UNTIL **YOU** CAME ALONG.

THAT PICTURE'S OF MY FAMILY . . . BEFORE. IT WAS RAINY.

MY PARENTS WENT FOR A DRIVE AND . . . WELL . . .

OUR FAMILY'S LITTLE NOW . . . BUT YOU COULD BE PART OF IT.

'OHANA MEANS FAMILY. FAMILY MEANS NOBODY GETS LEFT BEHIND.

BUT IF YOU WANT TO LEAVE, YOU CAN. I'LL REMEMBER YOU, THOUGH.

STITCH LEFT LILO'S ROOM. HE OPENED HER BOOK AND BEGAN TO READ.

BACK IN OUTER SPACE, THE COUNCILWOMAN WAS REGRETTING HER DECISION TO SEND JUMBA AND PLEAKLEY TO EARTH.

IT SEEMS I HAVE OVERESTIMATED JUMBA AND PLEAKLEY. CATCHING 626 COULD BE YOUR REDEMPTION, CAPTAIN GANTU. WHEN CAN YOU LEAVE?

NOW.

AND BACK ON EARTH, JUMBA AND PLEAKLEY WERE ABOUT TO GET PINK SLIPS THROUGH THEIR COMMUNICATOR.

THIS IS THE GRAND COUNCILWOMAN SPEAKING. JUMBA, PLEAKLEY . . . YOU'RE FIRED.

FINE! NOW WE DO IT MY WAY.

OH NO!

BUT JUMBA WAS *GOING* TO DO IT HIS WAY, WHETHER PLEAKLEY LIKED IT OR NOT!

STITCH HAD TURNED SCRUMP INTO ONE POWERFUL FIRECRACKER!

THE BATTLE RAGED ON, AND FINALLY LILO CALLED COBRA BUBBLES FOR HELP. MEANWHILE, NANI HEADED HOME FROM HER INTERVIEW, WHICH—WITHOUT STITCH THERE TO GUM THINGS UP—HAD GONE REAL WELL. UNFORTUNATELY, THE SAME COULDN'T BE SAID FOR THE SITUATION AT HOME!

OH, NO.

KABLOOOM!

WHEN NANI GOT HOME, SHE FOUND SHE WASN'T THE ONLY ONE WHO HAD JUST ARRIVED ON THE SCENE! COBRA BUBBLES WAS THERE, TOO!

. . . AND THEN THE BIG ALIEN—

LILO!

NO! YOU'RE **NOT** TAKING HER! I'M THE ONLY FAMILY SHE HAS!

IT'S CLEAR TO ME THAT YOU NEED **HER** A LOT MORE THAN SHE NEEDS **YOU**. I MEAN, IS **THIS** REALLY WHAT SHE NEEDS? LILO . . .

LILO?

LILO!

LILO HAD GONE TO FIND STITCH. AND WHEN SHE DID, HE TRANSFORMED BACK INTO HIS REAL SELF—ANTENNAE AND ALL. BUT UNFORTUNATELY, LILO WASN'T THE ONLY ONE WHO HAD FOUND STITCH.

AND I THOUGHT YOU'D BE **TOUGH** TO CATCH.

WR-R-R-R

LILO!

LILO!

KRR-RR-OOM!

GANTU HAD ACCIDENTALLY CAPTURED LILO INSTEAD. AND STITCH FELL TO THE GROUND.

NANI WANTED ANSWERS. AND SHE WANTED THEM NOW!

WHERE'S LILO? TALK! I KNOW YOU CAN!

OKAY, OKAY.

ENOUGH TALK! YOU'RE UNDER ARREST!

GALACTIC COMMAND? EXPERIMENT 626 IS IN CUSTODY! WE'VE SAVED THE DAY!

UH-OH. DON'T INTERACT WITH THE HUMAN.

WH-WHERE'S LILO?

WHO?

LILO. MY SISTER. YOU KNOW HER. PLEASE . . . PLEASE BRING HER BACK.

I'M SO SORRY. WE CAN'T. GALACTIC REGULATIONS.

'OHANA. MEANS FAMILY.

FAMILY MEANS . . .

NOBODY GETS LEFT BEHIND . . .

HMM?

WHAT? YOU THINK WE **WALKED** HERE?

THE GANG HOPPED IN JUMBA'S SHIP AND GOT GOING!

COUNCILWOMAN, I THOUGHT YOU'D LIKE TO KNOW ABOUT EXPERIMENT 626.

YES? YES? WHERE IS IT?

IT'S OVER THERE, IN— WHAT? BUT . . . NO! IMPOSSIBLE! HE—

CAPTAIN GANTU! WHAT'S—

GANTU HADN'T REALIZED HE'D CAPTURED LILO INSTEAD OF STITCH.

AND SO HE WAS SURPRISED TO SEE HIM FLYING IN JUMBA'S SHIP!

I'LL CALL YOU BACK.

SO . . . WHAT ARE WE DOING?

DON'T WORRY—WE ARE PRO-FESSIONALS.

626! GET THAT OUT OF YOUR MOUTH!

VEEERSSH!

SMASH!

YAI!

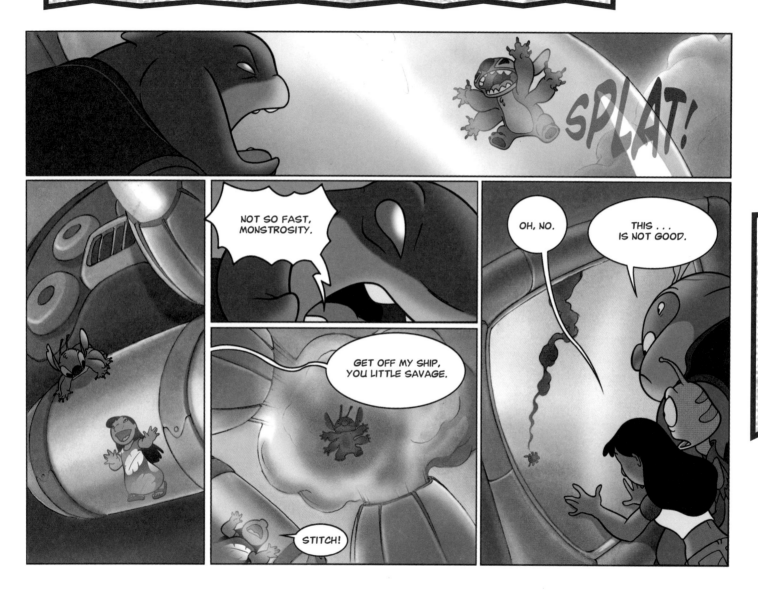

NOT SO FAST, MONSTROSITY.

GET OFF MY SHIP, YOU LITTLE SAVAGE.

STITCH!

OH, NO.

THIS . . . IS NOT GOOD.

SPLAT!

STITCH WAS ZAPPED BY GANTU AND HE FELL TO EARTH!

BUT GANTU WASN'T ABOUT TO LET HIM GO THAT EASILY.

RIBBIT.

EXPERIMENT 626 LOCATED.

ROWR!

HEH.

AHH!

ONCE STITCH MADE SURE THE DRIVER OF THE TRUCK WAS SAFE, HE GOT IN AND DROVE . . .

... RIGHT INTO A POOL OF MOLTEN LAVA!

WHOOOSH!

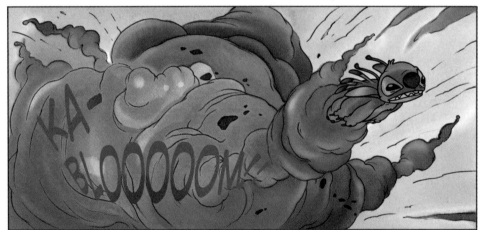

KA-BLOOOOOM!

THE EXPLODING TRUCK MADE STITCH FLY!

SMASH!

BOZO-HEAD.

DISGUSTING ABOMINATION.

STITCH HAD HAD ENOUGH OF GANTU.

STITCH JUMPED OFF GANTU'S EXPLODING SHIP, WITH LILO IN HIS ARMS!

WOW, COOL!

SWOOOSSSH!

AND AS FOR DAVID, WHO HAD BEEN SURFING THIS WHOLE TIME, HE DIDN'T KNOW **WHAT** HE WAS IN FOR.

DAVID, CAN YOU GIVE US A RIDE TO SHORE?

UH . . . SURE. BUT I'LL NEED TO MAKE TWO TRIPS.

WE HAVE 626!

TAKE IT TO MY SHIP.

YOU LEAVE HIM ALONE!

HOLD ON.

I THINK I SHOULD BE GOING NOW . . .

JUMBA, **YOU** ARE THE CAUSE OF ALL THIS! IF IT WASN'T FOR **YOUR** EXPERIMENT 626, NONE OF THIS—

STITCH.

MY NAME STITCH.

WHAT?

STITCH.

STITCH.

WHO ARE YOU?

THIS IS MY FAMILY. I FOUND IT. IT IS LITTLE AND BROKEN, BUT STILL GOOD. YEAH . . . STILL GOOD.

LILO, DON'T YOU HAVE A LICENSE FOR HIM?

YEAH! I PAID FOR IT AT THE SHELTER! WITH MY OWN MONEY . . . SORT OF . . . SO YOU'RE **STEALING** IF YOU TAKE STITCH!

AND RULES ARE RULES.

HMM. VERY WELL. THIS CREATURE HAS BEEN SENTENCED TO LIFE IN EXILE, WHICH SHALL BE HENCEFORTH SERVED HERE ON EARTH. THIS FAMILY IS NOW UNDER THE OFFICIAL PROTECTION OF THE UNITED GALACTIC FEDERATION.

DON'T LET THOSE TWO GET ON MY SHIP.

SO THAT'S THAT. NOW . . . ABOUT YOUR HOUSE . . .

IT'S AMAZING, THE THINGS YOU CAN DO WITH HOUSES THESE DAYS . . . WHEN YOU'VE GOT A COUPLE OF SLIGHTLY MAD ALIENS WORKING FOR YOU, WATCHED OVER BY THE UNIVERSE'S TOUGHEST SOCIAL WORKER.

AND WHEN THEY WERE DONE, IT WASN'T JUST A HOUSE THEY HAD BUILT. IT WAS A *HOME*. FOR NANI. FOR LILO. FOR STITCH . . .

. . . FOR A *FAMILY*.

'OHANA. IT'S A BEAUTIFUL THING.

THE END.

ALL THIS HAS HAPPENED BEFORE . . . AND IT WILL ALL HAPPEN AGAIN. BUT THIS TIME IT HAPPENED IN THE DARLINGS' HOUSE ON A QUIET STREET IN LONDON . . .

SAY YOUR PRAYERS, PETER PAN!

SPEAK FOR YOURSELF, CAPTAIN HOOK!

THE DARLING BROTHERS WERE PERFORMING AN ANCIENT CHILDHOOD RITUAL: **JUMPING** ON BEDS RATHER THAN **SLEEPING** IN THEM.

I'VE GOT YOU NOW!

LOOK, JOHN! **THERE'S** OUR TREASURE MAP! FATHER HAS IT!

MR. DARLING
DIDN'T KNOW
WHAT MICHAEL
WAS TALKING
ABOUT.

WHAT TREAS–AIEE!
MY SHIRT!

YAY!

THEN HE
FOUND OUT!
AND HE WAS
NONE TOO
HAPPY.

IT'S FROM THE
STORY WENDY
TOLD US!

WENDY?!

YOU'VE GONE TOO FAR
WITH THESE SILLY STORIES. THIS
SHALL BE YOUR LAST NIGHT IN
THE NURSERY!
IT'S TIME FOR YOU
TO GROW UP.

WHAT?

NO!

WENDY DIDN'T WANT TO LEAVE THE NURSERY. AND LATER SHE SPOKE WITH HER MOTHER.

MOTHER . . . I DON'T **WANT** TO GROW UP.

DON'T WORRY ABOUT IT ANYMORE TONIGHT.

SIGH . . .

THEY'RE **NOT** SILLY STORIES, YOU KNOW, MOTHER. THEY'RE **NOT**.

MRS. DARLING MOVED TOWARD THE WINDOW TO CLOSE AND LOCK IT FOR THE EVENING.

WHO?

WHY, **PETER PAN**, OF COURSE. I FOUND HIS SHADOW. I'M SURE HE'LL WANT IT BACK.

HIS SHADOW? HMM . . . YES, GOOD NIGHT, CHILDREN.

MRS. DARLING DIDN'T BELIEVE FOR A SECOND THAT PETER PAN *HAD* BEEN IN THE ROOM— MUCH LESS *LEFT HIS SHADOW* THERE!

BUT, AS MR. AND MRS. DARLING STEPPED OUT FOR THE EVENING, MRS. DARLING TRIED TO MAKE THE CASE FOR POOR WENDY. SHE KNEW HER DAUGHTER REALLY WANTED TO STAY IN THE NURSERY WITH HER BROTHERS!

GEORGE, ARE YOU SURE WENDY'S READY TO MOVE INTO HER OWN ROOM? SHE'S STILL SO YOUNG.

NONSENSE. I WAS ON MY OWN AT THAT AGE, AND JUST LOOK AT ME! YOU DON'T SEE ME TALKING ABOUT LOST SHADOWS, DO YOU?

WENDY'S FATHER WASN'T BUYING IT.

76

ABOVE THE HOUSE, A MYSTERIOUS FIGURE WAITED FOR THE OLDER DARLINGS TO LEAVE.

THEN, HE MADE HIS MOVE!

OKAY, TINK—
FIND MY SHADOW!

PETER PAN AND HIS FRIEND, THE FAIRY TINKER BELL, LOOKED ALL OVER THE NURSERY. BUT THEY COULDN'T FIND PETER'S SHADOW!

NO SIGN OF IT?
KEEP LOOKING!

THOSE PESKY SHADOWS—THEY'RE ALWAYS IN THE *LAST PLACE* YOU LOOK!

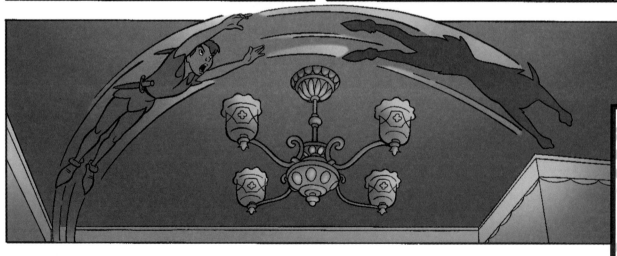

OF COURSE, *FINDING A SHADOW IS* ONLY HALF THE BATTLE . . .

I JUST *KNEW* YOU'D COME BACK!

PETER WAS HAPPY TO HAVE HIS SHADOW BACK, BUT HE DIDN'T KNOW HOW TO REATTACH IT!

OH! YOU CAN'T STICK IT ON WITH SOAP!

IT NEEDS SEWING. THAT'S THE **PROPER** WAY.

I KNEW YOU'D RETURN FOR YOUR SHADOW.

AND TO HEAR THE END OF YOUR **STORY**!

BUT . . . THAT WAS ALL ABOUT **YOU**!

EXACTLY! THAT'S WHAT I **LIKED** ABOUT IT!

OH! HA!

WENDY TOLD PETER THAT IT WAS HER LAST NIGHT IN THE NURSERY. AND SO THERE WOULD BE NO MORE STORIES. BUT PETER HAD A SOLUTION!

COME TO NEVER LAND—WHERE NO ONE *EVER* GROWS UP!

PETER, THAT WOULD BE SO WONDERFUL. BUT . . .

. . . BUT WHAT WOULD **MOTHER** SAY?

WHAT'S A "MOTHER"?

WENDY TOLD PETER THAT A MOTHER WAS WONDERFUL. SHE LOVED AND CHERISHED YOU, AND TOLD YOU BEDTIME STORIES.

PETER WAS HAPPY TO KNOW WHAT A MOTHER WAS, AND EXCITED TO TAKE WENDY BACK TO NEVER LAND. AFTER ALL, SHE WAS WONDERFUL AND TOLD GREAT STORIES, TOO!

LET'S GO!

OH . . . I'M SO HAPPY . . . I . . . I THINK I'LL GIVE YOU A KISS!

GULP!

*SMOOCH*SMOOCH*

!

TINKER BELL HEARD WHAT WAS GOING ON FROM INSIDE THE DRAWER SHE'D FALLEN INTO . . .

AND WENDY SOON FOUND OUT WHAT HAPPENS WHEN YOU MAKE A FAIRY JEALOUS!

TINK!

OW!!!

82

TINKER BELL HAD GOTTEN PETER VERY UPSET! HE CHASED HER AROUND THE ROOM, AND WOKE THE BOYS UP IN THE PROCESS.

PETER
WANTED
TO TAKE
WENDY TO
NEVER LAND
ALONE.
BUT WENDY
EXPLAINED
THAT SHE
COULDN'T
GO WITHOUT
HER
BROTHERS!

MAYBE FLYING WASN'T SO EASY. PETER DECIDED THAT THE DARLINGS NEEDED SOMETHING TO HELP THEM. THEN HE DISCOVERED WHAT!

OH, OF COURSE, FAIRY DUST!

SPRINKLE LIKE SO . . . AND VOILA!

FLYING FELT SO FREE AND EASY! NOW THEY JUST NEEDED PETER TO TELL THEM HOW TO GET TO NEVER LAND.

AND SUDDENLY LONDON TOWN DISAPPEARED FROM BENEATH THEM AND THE CHILDREN FOUND THEMSELVES IN A WHOLE NEW PLACE.

AND ON THE WATERS OF THAT WONDERFUL NEW PLACE, THERE WAS A NOT-SO-WONDERFUL SHIP. AND A PRETTY MEAN CAPTAIN WAS AT THE HELM!

THE PIRATE WAS CAPTAIN HOOK! HE WAS ON DECK WITH HIS SIDEKICK, MR. SMEE. AND HE WAS NOT VERY FOND OF PETER. NOT VERY FOND OF HIM *AT ALL*!

WE'VE SEARCHED **EVERYWHERE,** SMEE! I *MUST* FIND HIM AND HAVE MY REVENGE!

ARR . . .

EVER SINCE PETER PAN TOOK MY HAND AND FED IT TO THAT CROCODILE . . .

. . . THE MONSTER KEEPS COMING BACK FOR MORE!

CAPTAIN HOOK LOOKED OVER THE DECK. THE CROCK WAS THERE WAITING, AS USUAL.

WHY MUST HE TAUNT ME SO, SMEE?

JUST CALM DOWN, CAPTAIN.

PETER PAN! AHOY!

AT LAST! REVENGE SHALL BE MINE!

WE'VE GOT 'IM FOR SURE, CAP'N.

ALL HANDS ON DECK!

PREPARE TO FIRE.

PETER, WENDY, AND HER BROTHERS HAD LANDED ON A CLOUD, WHERE PETER PAN SHOWED THEM NEVER LAND!

WELL, WE'RE HERE!

OH, LOOK! MERMAID LAGOON! JUST AS I'VE ALWAYS DREAMED!

AND OVER THERE, THE INDIANS' CAMP!

AND CAPTAIN HOOK'S BOAT!

THEN, FROM THE BOAT, CAME AN UNEXPECTED SURPRISE!

INCOMING! EVERYONE DOWN!

TINK! TAKE WENDY AND THE BOYS TO THE ISLAND WHILE I DRAW HOOK'S FIRE!

TINKER BELL WAS VERY JEALOUS OF WENDY. SHE DIDN'T WANT TO HELP HER AT ALL!

TINKER BELL! NOT SO FAST, PLEASE! WE CAN'T KEEP UP!

SO LOSING THE DARLINGS— ESPECIALLY WENDY—WAS *EXACTLY* TINKER BELL'S PLAN!

WELL, IT WAS THE *FIRST* PART OF HER PLAN, ANYWAY . . .

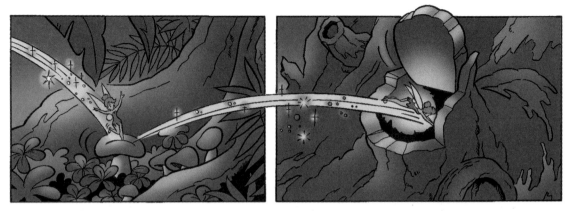

TINKER BELL WOKE UP PETER'S CREW, THE LOST BOYS, AND GOT READY TO PUT THE **SECOND** PART OF HER PLAN INTO ACTION!

♪♫!!

HEY, TINK— YOU'RE BACK! WHERE'S PETER?

A . . . A WHAT? A "WENDY-BIRD"?

YOU SAY PETER WANTS US TO SHOOT IT DOWN?

COOL! UM . . . WHAT'S A WENDY-BIRD?

LET'S FOLLOW TINK—SHE'LL SHOW US!

ERG.

LET'S GO!

THE LOST BOYS RAN OUT OF THEIR HIDEOUT. TINKER BELL POINTED TO WENDY, WHO WAS FLYING ABOVE THEM, AND THE LOST BOYS GOT READY TO SHOOT HER DOWN!

THANKFULLY, PETER WAS THERE TO SAVE WENDY.

GOOD HEAVENS.

PETER! YOU SAVED MY LIFE!

PETER PAN!

DID YOU SEE US?

NICE SHOT, HUH?

YOU BLOCKHEADS! I BRING YOU A **MOTHER** AND YOU SHOOT HER DOWN?

A . . . A MOTHER?

BUT TINK SAID YOU WANTED US TO **SHOOT** THE WENDY-BIRD!

UH-OH. TINKER BELL WAS IN T-R-O-U-B-L-E!

TINKER BELL TOLD YOU TO?

TINKER BELL, I HEREBY BANISH YOU FOREVER!

OH, PETER, NOT **FOREVER**!

WELL, FOR A WEEK, THEN. COME ON, WENDY, I'LL SHOW YOU AROUND!

OF COURSE, TINKER BELL WAS *NOT* HAPPY ABOUT ANY OF THIS.

THE BOYS FOUND THEMSELVES AMBUSHED, CAPTURED, AND TIED UP . . .

. . . BUT AT LEAST THEY GOT TO VISIT THE INDIANS' VILLAGE.

THE INDIAN CHIEF GREETED THE BOYS.

MEANWHILE, PETER AND WENDY WERE CHECKING OUT MERMAID LAGOON. THEN AN UNEXPECTED VISITOR SAILED BY!

WHAT'S GOING ON?

IT'S HOOK! AND HE'S CAPTURED PRINCESS TIGER LILY!

AS HOOK'S BOAT SAILED TOWARD SKULL ROCK, PETER DECIDED TO CHECK OUT THE SITUATION.

LET'S SEE WHAT THEY'RE UP TO.

HEAR ME NOW, MY DEAREST LITTLE PRINCESS . . .

PETER HID BEHIND A ROCK WHERE HE COULDN'T BE SPOTTED AND HE PRETENDED TO BE A GREAT SPIRIT!

AS HOOK AND SMEE TRIED TO ESCAPE THE KILLER CROC, PETER FLEW BACK TO WENDY.

WHAT ABOUT TIGER LILY?

TIGER . . . ? **OH!** TIGER LILY!

TIGER LILY!

PETER RUSHED TO TIGER LILY AND SAVED HER FROM DROWNING! THEN PETER AND WENDY RETURNED TIGER LILY TO HER FATHER.

THANK YOU FOR SAVING PRINCESS TIGER LILY. NOW, LET US CELEBRATE!

MUSIC PLAYED. EVERYONE DANCED. AND IT LOOKED LIKE TIGER LILY HAD A BIG, BAD *CRUSH* ON PETER!

NO PROBLEM, CHIEF. NOW, MAY I HAVE THIS DANCE?

WELL.

LILY'S CRUSH DIDN'T MAKE WENDY TOO HAPPY.

IF THAT'S HOW IT IS WITH THOSE TWO, I'M JUST GOING HOME.

MEANWHILE, AS TINKER BELL SAT ALONE, BANISHED FOR TRYING TO HURT WENDY, SMEE SNUCK UP BEHIND HER!

SMEE KIDNAPPED TINKER BELL AND BROUGHT HER TO HOOK'S SHIP.

BEGGING YOUR PARDON, TINKER BELL, BUT THE CAPTAIN WOULD LIKE A WORD WITH YOU!

♪♫!!!

RUMOR HAS IT WENDY HAS **ALREADY** COME BETWEEN YOU AND PETER.

CAPTAIN HOOK REALLY KNEW HOW TO PLAY UP TO TINKER BELL'S FEELINGS FOR PETER TO GET WHAT HE WANTED.

WE MUSTN'T JUDGE PETER TOO HARSHLY, DEAR. IT'S THAT **WENDY** WHO'S TO BLAME.

IF SOMETHING ISN'T DONE ABOUT HER, SHE WILL RUIN EVERYTHING! WE MUST SAVE PETER. BUT HOW CAN WE FIND HIM?

TINKER BELL WAS, OF COURSE, ALL FOR GETTING WENDY OUT OF THE PICTURE. SO SHE OFFERED TO HELP.

TINKER BELL SHOWED HOOK THE WAY TO PETER'S HIDEOUT.

BUT SHE WANTED TO MAKE SURE PETER WOULDN'T BE HURT. IT WAS WENDY WHO SHE WANTED TO GET LOST.

OF COURSE, OF COURSE—I PROMISE TO LAY NEITHER FINGER **NOR** HOOK ON PETER PAN.

ONCE TINKER BELL HAD CAPTAIN HOOK'S WORD THAT PETER WOULD NOT BE HARMED, SHE FINISHED MAPPING THE COURSE. BUT WHEN SHE WAS DONE SPILLING THE BEANS, HOOK TURNED AROUND AND LOCKED HER UP!

THANK YOU, MY DEAR. YOU'VE BEEN **MOST** HELPFUL.

WHAT A DASTARDLY VILLAIN, THAT HOOK!

BACK AT THE HANGMAN'S TREE, EVERYONE WAS TALKING ABOUT HOW MUCH FUN THEY'D HAD AT THE INDIANS' CELEBRATION FOR THE RETURN OF TIGER LILY!

I'M CHIEF PETER! GREETINGS, MOTHER WENDY!
WENDY WAS NOT IN THE MOOD.
DID CHIEF PETER HAVE FUN DANCING WITH TIGER LILY?
!
JOHN, MICHAEL, WE'RE GOING HOME.
OTHERWISE MOTHER WILL WORRY SO.
AREN'T YOU OUR MOTHER?
OF COURSE NOT. I MEAN OUR REAL MOTHER.
WHO'S SHE?

IT SEEMED AS IF *EVERYONE* WANTED TO SEE MOTHER.

SO DO WE! WE ALL WANT TO HAVE THAT MOTHER!

PETER HAD HEARD ENOUGH.

FINE! GO BACK AND GROW UP! BUT ONCE YOU DO, YOU CAN NEVER COME BACK. NEVER!

THAT *IS* TOO BAD. OH WELL!

THE LOST BOYS, JOHN, AND MICHAEL LEFT THE HIDEOUT.

THEY'LL BE BACK, I THINK.

WENDY WAS TERRIBLY SAD TO LEAVE PETER THIS WAY. SO, SHE TRIED TO AT LEAST SAY GOOD-BYE BEFORE SHE LEFT.

OH, PETER . . .

GOOD-BYE.

BUT AS SOON AS SHE LEFT THE HANGMAN'S TREE, SHE FOUND HERSELF IN DEEP TROUBLE!

!

UMPH!

WITH THE BOYS AND WENDY TIED UP, CAPTAIN HOOK WAS FREE TO CARRY OUT ANOTHER ONE OF HIS SINISTER PLANS.

NOW FOR PETER PAN.

COULDN'T YOU JUST FIGHT HIM WITH YOUR HANDS?

YES. BUT I GAVE MY WORD NOT TO TOUCH HIM. AND I *NEVER* BREAK A PROMISE!

CAPTAIN HOOK LOWERED A WRAPPED GIFT BOX DOWN INTO PETER'S HIDEOUT. A *TICKING* GIFT BOX!

THEN THE CAPTAIN AND HIS CREW TOOK THE BOYS AND WENDY TO HIS SHIP AND TIED THEM UP. AND HE MADE THEM AN OFFER. WELL . . . IT WAS REALLY MORE OF A DEMAND. THEY COULD JOIN HIS CREW . . . OR WALK THE PLANK.

BUT WENDY HAD DIFFERENT IDEAS. SHE TOLD THEM THEY WOULD NOT SIGN UP FOR THE CREW OR WALK THE PLANK! PETER PAN WOULD SAVE THEM!

CAPTAIN HOOK EXPLAINED THAT THE BOX HE HAD LEFT PETER HAD A BOMB INSIDE IT! AND WHEN THE TIMER WENT OFF, PETER PAN WOULD BE BLASTED OUT OF NEVER LAND FOREVER!

TINKER BELL OVERHEARD THE CAPTAIN. AND SHE DID *NOT* LIKE WHAT SHE WAS HEARING.

SHE WAS THE ONLY ONE WHO COULD SAVE PETER! SHE MANAGED TO JERK HER LAMP OVER THE LEDGE AND ESCAPE!

TINKER BELL GRABBED THE BOX JUST IN TIME TO GET IT AWAY FROM PETER.

THE TERRIBLE EXPLOSION WAS MUSIC TO CAPTAIN HOOK'S EARS. HE THOUGHT PETER WAS DONE FOR.

AND SO PASSETH A WORTHY OPPONENT.

NOW . . . THE QUILL OR THE PLANK?

WE WILL **NEVER** JOIN YOUR CREW, CAPTAIN.

SHARKS AWAIT THEN, YOUNG LADY.

GOOD-BYE, BOYS.

WENDY JUMPED, AND CAPTAIN HOOK WAITED TO HEAR A SPLASH AS SHE FELL IN THE WATER. BUT IT NEVER CAME.

PETER HAD SAVED HER! AND HE HAD SAVED TINKER BELL FROM THE BLAST, TOO! NOW HE WAS READY TO *FIGHT*!

THE PIRATES ATTACKED, BUT THEY WERE NO MATCH FOR THE LOST BOYS!

WITH THE BAND OF PIRATES DEFEATED, CAPTAIN HOOK WAS LEFT ALONE TO DEAL WITH PETER PAN.

THIS TIME YOU'VE GONE TOO FAR!

OOF!

TAKE THAT!

WHOA!

HA!

AS PETER FELL, HE GRABBED A ROPE AND SWUNG RIGHT BACK UP TOWARD HOOK!

THE FIGHT WENT ON FOR WHAT SEEMED LIKE HOURS.

WHILE A CERTAIN CROCODILE WAITED HUNGRILY DOWN BELOW!

FINALLY, CAPTAIN HOOK TRIPPED UP! AND THE CROCODILE GOT THE MEAL HE'D BEEN WAITING FOR!

THE BOYS, PETER, WENDY, AND EVEN TINKER BELL CELEBRATED! CAPTAIN HOOK WAS DONE FOR! AND PETER WAS READY TO TAKE WENDY AND HER BROTHERS BACK HOME TO LONDON!

HOOK'S SHIP SET SAIL AND FLEW AWAY, BRINGING THE DARLINGS BACK TO LONDON. AND BACK AT HOME, WENDY WAS READY TO GROW UP. BUT SHE NEVER FORGOT THE ADVENTURES SHE HAD WITH PETER AND THE LOST BOYS IN NEVER LAND!

THE END

Once upon a time, in a far-off galaxy, there lived a boy named Jim Hawkins. Jim loved reading tales about the infamous pirate Captain Flint and the legendary Treasure Planet. Until the time came when he found himself in the middle of just such a tale . . .

. . . BUT WE'RE GETTING AHEAD OF OURSELVES. SO LET'S START ON JIM'S HOME PLANET OF MONTRESSOR, WHERE JIM LIKED NOTHING MORE THAN TO RIDE HIS SOLAR WINDSURFER IN THOSE PLACES HE FELT MOST FREE—

YAHOOOO!

VRROOOOM!

RRROARR

—THOSE PLACES WHERE WINDSURFING **ISN'T** ALLOWED.

PULL OVER IMMEDIATELY.

OH, GREAT.

MEANWHILE, JIM'S MOTHER WAS HARD AT WORK OVER AT THE HOMEY BENBOW INN, WHICH SHE OWNED AND RAN.

SORRY, DELBERT. IT'S BEEN CRAZY HERE ALL MORNING.

NO PROBLEM, SARAH. HOW'S JIM?

MUCH BETTER, THANKS.

WELL, THAT'S GOOD TO HEAR. NO MORE, ER . . . ?

NO, NO TROUBLE, REALLY. I THINK HE'S TURNED A CORNER.

SUDDENLY, THE DOOR SWUNG OPEN, REVEALING TWO ROBOT CONSTABLES . . . AND THEY HAD JIM WITH THEM! THIS COULD *NOT* BE GOOD.

MRS. HAWKINS?

JIM!

I THINK HE TURNED THE **WRONG** CORNER!

THE ROBOT CONSTABLES HAD BAD NEWS FOR JIM'S MOM.

WE APPREHENDED YOUR SON OPERATING A SOLAR VEHICLE IN A RESTRICTED AREA. THIS IS A VIOLATION OF HIS PAROLE.

BAD MOVE.

THE CONSTABLES TOLD JIM'S MOTHER THAT THE NEXT TIME JIM WAS CAUGHT DOING SOMETHING WRONG, THEY WOULD PUT HIM IN JAIL! AND LATER, WHILE JIM WAITED OUTSIDE, HIS MOM TALKED TO HER FRIEND DR. DOPPLER ABOUT THE SITUATION.

I'M AT THE END OF MY ROPE. EVER SINCE HIS FATHER LEFT, I'VE COMPLETELY LOST CONTROL OF JIM.

I DON'T KNOW WHAT TO SAY, SARAH.

JIM WAS UPSET ABOUT THE SITUATION. BUT AS BAD AS IT WAS, HE WAS ABOUT TO LEARN THAT IT WASN'T HIS *ONLY* PROBLEM. A PIRATE SHIP SUDDENLY FELL FROM THE SKY AND CRASHED RIGHT IN FRONT OF HIM!

JIM KNEW THAT THE PIRATE NEEDED HELP. THERE WAS ONLY ONE THING TO DO. AND HIS MOM WAS NOT GOING TO LIKE IT ONE BIT . . .

JIM BROUGHT THE PIRATE, WHO WAS CALLED BILLY BONES, BACK TO HIS HOME.

MOM, HE'S REALLY HURT.

THE CHEST, LAD.

HE'LL BE HERE SOON . . . CAN'T LET HIM FIND THIS . . .

WHO?

THE CYBORG! BEWARE . . . THE CYBORG!

RUMBLE RUMBLE

HUH?

UGH.

BILLY BONES COLLAPSED. SUDDENLY THE ROOM SHOOK AS SOMETHING HUGE LANDED OUTSIDE THE INN.

IT WAS A SPACE SCHOONER! AND IT WAS FILLED WITH PIRATES!

JIM KNEW THAT HE, HIS MOTHER, AND THE DOCTOR NEEDED TO GET OUT OF THERE FAST.

WE GOTTA GO!

KERRASH!

I BELIEVE I'M WITH JIM ON THIS ONE!

THEY ESCAPED JUST AS THE PIRATE CREW EMERGED FROM THE SHIP LOOKING FOR THE SPHERE THAT HAD BEEN GIVEN TO JIM.

WHILE THE PIRATES SACKED THE INN, JIM AND HIS MOM MANAGED TO ESCAPE TO DR. DOPPLER'S HOUSE.

WHILE THE DOCTOR DELIVERED THE BAD NEWS TO JIM'S MOM, JIM WAS NERVOUSLY FIDGETING WITH THE SPHERE BILLY BONES HAD GIVEN HIM. AND THEN SOMETHING AMAZING HAPPENED.

AN AWFUL LOT OF TROUBLE OVER THAT ODD LITTLE SPHERE. THOSE MARKINGS ARE BAFFLING. IT WOULD TAKE YEARS TO UNLOCK—HEY!

WHY . . . THIS IS SOME SORT OF MAP! WAIT, WAIT—THAT'S US! THAT'S THE PLANET MONTRESSOR!

JIM HAD SOMEHOW ACCESSED A MAP WITHIN THE SPHERE. DR. DOPPLER STARTED TO READ IT.

DR. DOPPLER EXPLAINED THAT HE WOULD PAY FOR THE TRIP, GET A SHIP, AND HIRE A CAPTAIN AND CREW. JIM'S MOM WAS STILL TOTALLY AGAINST THE IDEA. BUT THAT DIDN'T MEAN JIM WASN'T GOING TO CONTINUE TO TRY AND CONVINCE HER.

MOM, LOOK—THIS IS MY CHANCE TO PROVE I'M NOT A LOSER.

SARAH, IF I MAY . . . ?

YOU SAID YOU'VE TRIED EVERYTHING. THERE ARE WORSE THINGS THAN A FEW CHARACTER-BUILDING MONTHS IN SPACE.

JIM . . . I DON'T WANT TO LOSE YOU.

YOU WON'T. EVER.

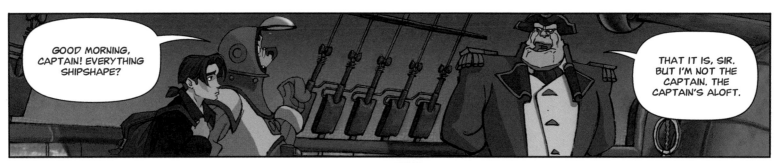

JIM'S MOM FINALLY LET HIM GO. AND BEFORE LONG, DR. DOPPPLER, IN HIS CLUNKY SPACE SUIT, AND JIM BOARDED THEIR SHIP . . . THE RLS *LEGACY!*

GOOD MORNING, CAPTAIN! EVERYTHING SHIPSHAPE?

THAT IT IS, SIR. BUT I'M NOT THE CAPTAIN. THE CAPTAIN'S ALOFT.

THE DOCTOR HAD MISTAKEN MR. ARROW, WHO WAS THE FIRST MATE, FOR THE CAPTAIN. BUT NOW HE AND JIM WERE ABOUT TO MEET THE *REAL* CAPTAIN, CAPTAIN AMELIA!

MISTER ARROW! I'VE CHECKED THIS MISERABLE SHIP FROM STEM TO STERN AND, AS USUAL, IT'S SPOT-ON. CAN YOU GET **NOTHING** WRONG?

YOU FLATTER ME, CAPTAIN.

AH, DR. DOPPLER, I PRESUME.

WHY, YES!

I'M CAPTAIN AMELIA, LATE OF A FEW NASTY RUN-INS WITH THE PROCYAN ARMADA. YOU'VE MET MY FIRST OFFICER, MISTER ARROW—STERLING, TOUGH, HONEST, BRAVE, AND TALL.

THE CAPTAIN ASKED THE DOCTOR AND JIM TO COME TO HER STATEROOM SO THEY COULD TALK FURTHER. SHE TOLD THEM NOT TO TALK ABOUT THE MAP IN FRONT OF THE CREW MEMBERS. SHE ASKED THEM FOR THE MAP AND LOCKED IT UP IN HER STATEROOM SAFE. THEN SHE EXPLAINED *WHY* SHE WAS BEING SO CAREFUL.

LET ME MAKE THIS AS SIMPLE AS POSSIBLE. I DON'T CARE FOR THE CREW YOU'VE HIRED. THEY ARE—HOW DID I DESCRIBE THEM, ARROW?

A LUDICROUS PILE OF DRIVELING GALOOTS, MA'AM.

NOW SEE HERE!

DR. DOPPLER WAS LEARNING QUICKLY THAT CAPTAIN AMELIA DID NOT MINCE WORDS. *OR* ACTIONS!

MISTER ARROW, ESCORT THESE TWO DOWN TO THE GALLEY. YOUNG HAWKINS WILL BE WORKING FOR OUR COOK.

WHAT? THE COOK?

SOON . . .

MISTER SILVER?

AH, MISTER ARROW, SIR. BRINGIN' DISTINGUISHED GENTS TO ME HUMBLE GALLEY.

HAD I KNOWN, I'D 'A TUCKED IN ME SHIRT.

GASP! A CYBORG.

MAY I INTRO- DUCE DR. DOPPLER AND JIM HAWKINS.

SILVER HANDED JIM AND DR. DOPPLER A BOWL OF... WELL... SOMETHING. THEN JIM NOTICED HIS SPOON WAS ACTING FUNNY!

AHA!

I SEE YOU'VE MET ME FRIEND!

WHAT IS HE?

WHAT IS HE?

HE'S A **MORPH**. RESCUED THE LITTLE SHAPE-SHIFTER ON PROTEUS ONE. BEEN TOGETHER EVER SINCE.

WELL, WE'RE ABOUT TO GET UNDERWAY. DO YOU WANT TO OBSERVE THE LAUNCH, DOCTOR?

WHY, OF COURSE! PLEASE!

JIM WAS IN TROUBLE. THIS ALIEN, CALLED SCROOP, WAS NASTY!
BUT JUST THEN, ARROW STOPPED BY TO SEE WHAT WAS GOING ON.

THERE'S **NO BRAWLING** ON THIS SHIP.

ANY FURTHER OFFENDERS WILL BE CONFINED TO THE BRIG FOR THE REMAINDER OF THE VOYAGE. AM I CLEAR, MISTER SCROOP?

TRANSPARENTLY.

JIMBO! I GAVE YOU A JOB TO DO!

MORPH, LET ME KNOW IF THIS PUP FINDS HIMSELF "DISTRACTED" AGAIN.

BUT SILVER HIMSELF SAW TO IT THAT JIM DID NOT BECOME DISTRACTED. FROM SCRAPING BARNACLES OFF THE SHIP TO SCRUBBING DISHES IN THE KITCHEN, THE COOK TAUGHT JIM WHAT IT TOOK TO KEEP A SHIP IN ORDER.

MISTER SILVER GREW EVER MORE IMPRESSED BY YOUNG JIM. AS A REWARD FOR ALL HIS HARD WORK, HE INVITED JIM OUT FOR A RIDE IN THE LONGBOAT. AND WHEN THEY RETURNED, SILVER AND JIM HAD A CHAT.

WISH I COULD'A HANDLED A SHIP AS WELL AS YOU WHEN I WAS A PUP.

THEY WEREN'T IMPRESSED BACK HOME. BUT THEY WILL BE.

THAT RIGHT?

LET'S JUST SAY I'VE GOT SOME PLANS THAT'LL MAKE FOLKS SEE ME A BIT DIFFERENTLY.

JIM LOOKED AT SILVER'S MECHANICAL HAND. SINCE THE FIRST DAY THEY'D MET, JIM HAD WONDERED HOW SILVER HAD BECOME A CYBORG.

HOW DID **THAT** HAPPEN?

SOMETIMES PLANS GO ASTRAY.

IS IT WORTH IT?

YOU GIVE UP SOME THINGS CHASIN' A DREAM.

CHART YOUR OWN COURSE. STICK WITH IT, AND YOU'LL BE ALL RIGHT, JIMBO.

JIM THOUGHT ABOUT WHAT SILVER HAD SAID. MAYBE THE OLD CYBORG WAS ON TO SOMETHING. THEN, SUDDENLY, THE SHIP BEGAN TO ROCK LIKE CRAZY!

THE COSMIC FORCE WAS SO GREAT THAT IT CAUSED THE CREW TO LOSE CONTROL OF THE SHIP! BUT WITH A LITTLE HELP FROM DR. DOPPLER, THE CAPTAIN DEVISED A PLAN.

THE WAVES! THEY'RE SO ERRATIC!

NO, CAPTAIN! THEY'RE NOT ERRATIC AT ALL! THERE'LL BE ANOTHER IN 47.2 SECONDS, FOLLOWED BY THE **BIGGEST** OF ALL!

BRILLIANT, DOCTOR! WE'LL RIDE THAT ONE **OUT** OF HERE!

ALL SAILS SECURED, CAPTAIN!

GOOD MAN. NOW **RELEASE** THEM.

UH . . . AYE, CAPTAIN. YOU HEARD HER, MEN— UNFURL THOSE SAILS!

BUT WE JUST FINISHED—

—TYIN' 'EM DOWN!

MISTER HAWKINS! ENSURE ALL LIFELINES ARE SECURED!

AYE-AYE, CAPTAIN!

LIFELINES SECURED!

THINGS SEEMED TO BE GOING GREAT...

THE HARDENED CREW THOUGHT THEY KNEW ALL ABOUT FAST SHIPS. BUT UNTIL YOU'VE GONE *SUPERNOVA*, YOU DON'T KNOW A *THING* ABOUT SPEED!

VAAWHOOOOSH!

FASCINATING!

HUZZAH!

THANK YOU FOR YOUR HELP, DOCTOR.

ALL HANDS ACCOUNTED FOR, MISTER ARROW?

ALL **BUT** MISTER ARROW, I'M AFRAID, CAPTAIN . . .

. . . HIS LIFE-LINE WASN'T SECURE.

NO! I CHECKED THEM ALL! I DID!

MISTER ARROW WAS A FINE SPACER, FINER THAN MOST OF US COULD EVER HOPE TO BE, BUT HE KNEW THE RISKS, AS DO WE ALL. RETURN TO YOUR POSTS.

JIM, LIKE CAPTAIN AMELIA, WAS REALLY UPSET, AND SILVER TRIED TO COMFORT HIM.

. . . IT WEREN'T YOUR FAULT, Y'KNOW. YOU WAS A WONDER WITH THOSE KNOTS. HALF THE CREW'D BE LOST IF NOT FOR YOU.

DON'T YOU GET IT? I THOUGHT THAT MAYBE I COULD DO SOMETHING RIGHT FOR ONCE. INSTEAD . . .

NOW, YOU LISTEN TO ME. YOU GOT GREATNESS INSIDE YOU. AND WHEN THE TIME COMES TO SHOW WHAT YOU'RE MADE OF . . . WELL, I HOPE I'M THERE TO SEE.

THERE, THERE, LAD. IT'S OKAY.

NOW, I, UH . . . BEST BE GETTIN' ABOUT ME WATCH, AND YOU'D BEST GET SOME SHUT-EYE.

THE NEXT MORNING, SILVER HAD A WORD WITH THE CREW. JIM WAS CLOSE BY, AND HE HID SO HE COULD LISTEN IN.

DISOBEY ME ORDERS AGAIN, LIKE THAT STUNT WITH MISTER ARROW, AND YOU'LL *JOIN* HIM, SCROOP.

YOU'VE A SOFT SPOT FOR THAT BOY, SILVER.

NOW, MARK MY WORDS. I CARE ABOUT **ONE** THING, AND ONE THING **ONLY**— FLINT'S TREASURE TROVE.

SILVER WAS A BAD GUY! A PIRATE! JIM FELT BETRAYED, HURT, AND USED. HOW COULD SILVER DO THIS?

CAPTAIN AMELIA GAVE JIM THE TREASURE MAP. BUT MORPH GRABBED IT AND TOOK OFF!

THE BOAT WAS HIT, AND THE CASTAWAY CREW CRASH-LANDED ON TREASURE PLANET!

CAPTAIN AMELIA TOLD JIM TO SEARCH THE AREA FOR A SAFE PLACE. SHE DIDN'T WANT TO BE CAUGHT BY THE PIRATES.

I HAVE NO IDEA WHERE TO START.

AS JIM WALKED CAUTIOUSLY AROUND THE ALIEN PLANET, HE WAS SUDDENLY ATTACKED!

OOH! THIS IS FANTASTIC! A CARBON-BASED LIFE-FORM COME TO RESCUE ME AT LAST!

I JUST WANNA HUG YOU AND SQUEEZE YOU—

OKAY, ALREADY! LET GO!

SORRY! I'VE BEEN MAROONED FOR SO LONG, AND AFTER THE FIRST HUNDRED YEARS, IT GETS LONELY!

JIM'S NEW BUDDY TOLD HIM HIS NAME WAS B.E.N. IT STOOD FOR BIO-ELECTRONIC NAVIGATOR. HE ALSO TOLD HIM THAT LONG AGO FLINT'S PIRATES HAD STOLEN HIS MIND. POOR FELLA!

B.E.N. TOOK JIM, THE CAPTAIN, THE DOCTOR, AND MORPH BACK TO HIS HOME IN A CAVE. THE DOCTOR NOTICED SOMETHING FAMILIAR ON THE WALLS.

EVERYONE KNEW THEY WERE ON TO SOMETHING. THE TREASURE MUST BE REALLY CLOSE NOW. BUT B.E.N. WAS ABOUT TO MAKE A *BIG* MISTAKE . . .

BLAM!

BANG!

PWIIING!

KAPOW!

HOLD YOUR FIRE!

JIMBO! IF IT'S ALL RIGHT WITH YOUR CAP'N, I'D LIKE A WORD WITH YOU.

THEY'VE COME TO BARGAIN FOR THE MAP, DOUBTLESSLY . . .

OH!

THAT MEANS . . . THEY THINK **WE'VE** STILL GOT IT.

JIM WENT TO MEET SILVER. BUT HE KNEW HE COULDN'T TRUST HIM AFTER ALL THAT HAD HAPPENED.

WHATEVER YOU HEARD BACK THERE ABOUT YOU—I DIDN'T MEAN A WORD OF IT. IF THAT LOT THOUGHT I'D GONE SOFT, THEY'D HAVE GUTTED US **BOTH**.

LISTEN, YOU GET ME THAT MAP, AND AN EVEN PORTION OF THE TREASURE'S YOURS.

YOU'RE REALLY SOMETHING. YOU TAUGHT ME ONE THING—"STICK TO IT." WELL, THAT'S WHAT I'M GOING TO DO. YOU'LL NEVER SEE ONE **DRUBLOON** OF MY TREASURE.

THAT TREASURE IS *MINE*!

TRY TO GET IT WITHOUT *MY* MAP, THEN!

EITHER I GET THAT MAP BY DAWN, OR I'LL USE THE SHIP'S CANNONS TO BLAST YA ALL TO KINGDOM COME!

SILVER RETURNED TO THE SHIP, AND JIM WENT BACK TO B.E.N.'S CAVE. HE NEEDED TO FIGURE OUT THE NEXT PART OF THE PLAN.

IF ONLY WE COULD GET TO THE SHIP. WITHOUT THAT MAP, WE'RE DEAD.

WE'RE DEAD! WE'RE DEAD!

LOOKS LIKE YOU COULD USE SOME QUIET TIME, JIMMY, SO I'LL JUST SLIP OUT THE BACK DOOR . . .

BACK DOOR?

NO, JIM! WAIT!

I'LL BE BACK!

JIM HAD FOUND A SAFE WAY OUT OF THE CAVE! HE ESCAPED THROUGH B.E.N.'S BACK DOOR AND HEADED FOR THE SHIP!

JIM AND B.E.N. MANAGED TO GET BACK TO THE *LEGACY.* NOW ALL THEY NEEDED TO DO WAS FIND THE TREASURE MAP!

OKAY, WE'RE ON BOARD. I'LL GET THE MAP. YOU WAIT HERE.

ROGER, JIMMY! I'LL NEUTRALIZE THE CANNONS, SIR!

WHAT? NO! B.E.N., WAIT!

WHAT'S THE BIG DEAL ABOUT DISABLING SOME CANNONS? I FIND ONE LITTLE WIRE AND— OH, MAMA!

THANKFULLY, JIM WAS HAVING MORE LUCK WITH HIS OWN TASK!

GOT IT!

BUT IF HE HADN'T FIGURED IT OUT YET, JIM WAS ABOUT TO DISCOVER THAT NOTHING EVER COMES *THAT* EASILY. ESPECIALLY WHEN YOU'RE TRAVELING WITH A ROBOT WHO ACCIDENTALLY TRIGGERS ALARMS!

AAAROOOOOOoo!

CABIN BOY.

OOH . . . SIREN BAD! BAD SIREN!

THAT ROBOT'S GONNA GET US KILLED.

SCROOP HAD HEARD THE SIREN AND FOUND JIM! THINGS WERE GETTING REAL UGLY, AND JIM RAN FOR HIS LIFE!

BUT SCROOP CAUGHT UP WITH HIM. THEY FOUGHT ON THE MAST, HANGING ON TO THE POLE AND FRAYING ROPE.

JIM WAS SAFE! AND WITH SCROOP GONE, HE WAS ABLE TO RUSH BACK TO THE CAPTAIN AND DR. DOPPLER WITH THE MAP!

DOC, I'M BACK! I'VE GOT THE MAP!

BUT THE DOCTOR AND THE CAPTAIN WERE NOT ALONE.

FINE WORK, JIMBO.

FINE WORK INDEED.

NOW. . .

CLICK!

OPEN IT, OR HE'S A GONER.

JIM OPENED THE MAP TO SAVE THE DOCTOR. A FANTASTIC GREEN RAY SHOT OUT FROM IT AND FORMED A PATH, POINTING THE WAY TO THE TREASURE!

OH MY . . . WOULD YOU LOOK AT THAT?

TIE HIM UP WITH THE OTHERS.

NOPE. YOU WANT THE MAP, YOU TAKE ME, TOO.

FINE. WE'LL TAKE 'EM ALL.

JIM OPENED THE MAP ONCE MORE. A CRYSTAL-CLEAR PATH SHOT FROM IT AGAIN, AND OFF THEY WENT IN SEARCH OF THE PROMISED TREASURE.

BUT THEY SOON FOUND THE TRAIL LED TO . . . NOWHERE!

HUH?

WHERE'D THE TRAIL GO? THERE'S NOTHING THERE!

THIS AIN'T NO TIME FOR GAMES, JIMBO.

I . . . I DON'T KNOW WHAT HAPPENED! IT JUST . . .

I KNEW THIS HUMAN WASN'T TRUSTWORTHY!

THEN JIM NOTICED SOMETHING . . .

THE MAP! IT FITS RIGHT INTO THIS CREVICE.

VWOOOOSH!

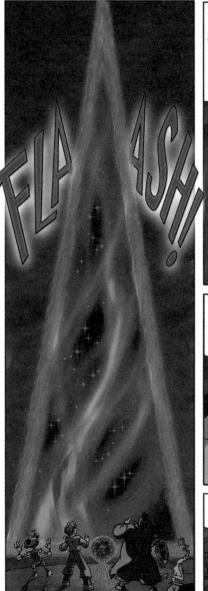

THAT'S THE LAGOON NEBULA, HALFWAY ACROSS THE GALAXY! **THAT'S** HOW CAPTAIN FLINT TRAVELED! HE USED THIS PORTAL TO ROAM THE UNIVERSE!

BUT WHERE'D HE STASH THE **TREASURE**?

JUST THEN, B.E.N. SEEMED TO HAVE A MOMENT OF CLARITY.

TREASURE . . . TREASURE? IT'S BURIED IN THE CENTROID OF THE MECHANISM!

WELL . . . WHAT IF THE **WHOLE PLANET** IS THE MECHANISM! THEN THE TREASURE'S IN THE CENTER OF THE PLANET!

BUT HOW DO WE GET THERE?

EASY—JUST OPEN A DOOR.

JIM TOUCHED A PICTURE OF TREASURE PLANET ON THE MAP, AND A DOOR OPENED TO THE INSIDE OF THE PLANET!

WHERE ARE WE NOW?

IN THE CORE OF TREASURE PLANET ITSELF! THANKS TO B.E.N., WE'RE IN THE CENTROID OF THE MECHANISM!

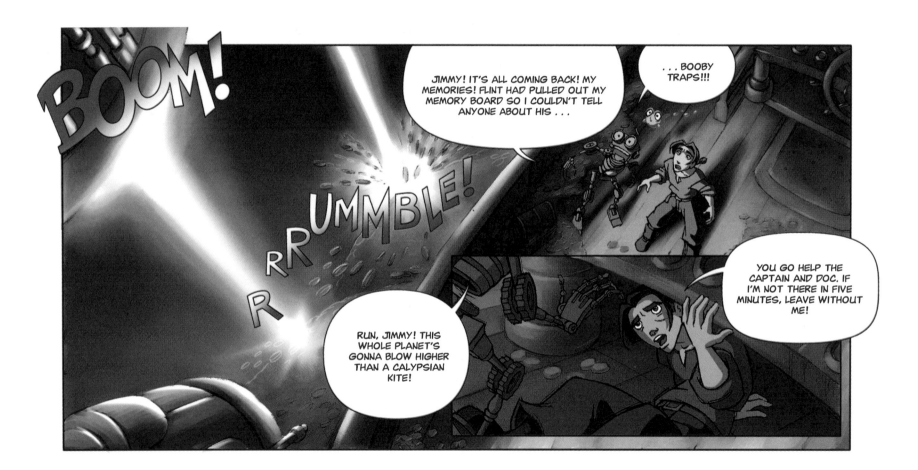

BOOM!

RRRUMMBLE!

JIMMY! IT'S ALL COMING BACK! MY MEMORIES! FLINT HAD PULLED OUT MY MEMORY BOARD SO I COULDN'T TELL ANYONE ABOUT HIS . . .

. . . BOOBY TRAPS!!!

RUN, JIMMY! THIS WHOLE PLANET'S GONNA BLOW HIGHER THAN A CALYPSIAN KITE!

YOU GO HELP THE CAPTAIN AND DOC. IF I'M NOT THERE IN FIVE MINUTES, LEAVE WITHOUT ME!

AS THE PLANET CONTINUED TO RUMBLE, THE TREASURE STARTED SLIPPING AWAY FROM SILVER.

CRACK!

RRRUMMMBLE!

NO! NO! PLEASE!

AH . . . JIMBO. EVER SO SMART YOU ARE.

JIM WAS UP AT THE HELM, TRYING TO FIX FLINT'S SHIP.

AND WHAT DO YOU KNOW... HE MANAGED TO DO IT!

YES! I GOT THE ENGINE RUNNING, MORPH! WE ARE **GONE**!

AH, JIMBO—THE SEVENTH WONDER OF THE UNIVERSE.

VROOM!

I LIKE YA SO MUCH, LAD... BUT I'VE COME TOO FAR TO LET ANYTHING STAND BETWEEN ME AND ME TREASURE.

GET BACK!

SLAAM!

AN ENERGY BEAM FROM THE EXPLODING PLANET SLICED THROUGH THE SHIP, AND JIM JUMPED! BUT SILVER WOULDN'T LET GO OF THE BOAT. HE WAS TRYING TO PULL THE SHIP TOWARD HIM!

THEN MORPH FLEW BY TO TELL SILVER THAT JIM WAS IN DANGER!

SILVER HAD TO MAKE A CHOICE. HE COULD SAVE JIM, OR HE COULD SAVE THE TREASURE.

NEVER LET IT BE SAID THAT PIRATES DON'T HAVE FEELINGS...
OR THAT THEY CAN NEVER LEARN TO CARE FOR SOMEONE!

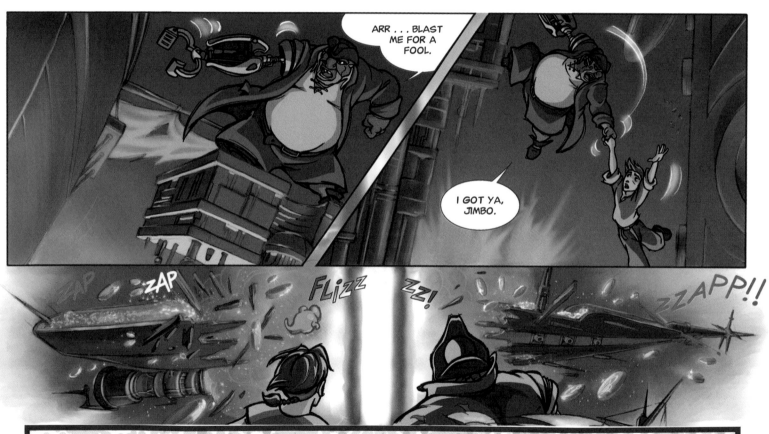

JUST LIKE THAT, THE LOOT OF A THOUSAND WORLDS WAS GONE. FOREVER.

JIM AND SILVER RAN THROUGH THE PORTAL AND BACK ONTO THE *LEGACY*. DR. DOPPLER AND CAPTAIN AMELIA HAD ESCAPED THEIR CAPTORS. AND THEY'D EVEN MANAGED TO DETAIN THE NASTY CREW OF PIRATES THAT HAD BEEN HOLDING THEM HOSTAGE.

SUDDENLY, A HUGE CHUNK OF DEBRIS FROM THE DOOMED PLANET FELL ON ONE OF THE SAILS, DESTROYING IT.

AH, CAP'N. YOU DROPPED FROM THE HEAVENS IN THE NICK O' TIME.

SAVE IT FOR THE JUDGE, SILVER.

CRACK!

WELL, THAT WASN'T GOOD. DAMAGE?

MIZZEN SAIL DEMOBILIZED, CAPTAIN. THRUSTERS AT THIRTY PERCENT OF CAPACITY.

CRASH!

THIRTY PERCENT? WE'LL NEVER CLEAR THE PLANET IN TIME!

JIM HAD AN IDEA.

TURN AROUND, THERE'S A PORTAL BACK THERE THAT CAN GET US OUT OF HERE.

LISTEN TO THE BOY! WHAT DO YOU NEED, JIMBO?

SILVER WELDED JIM A SURFBOARD, AND JIM TOOK OFF!

VROOOM!

JIM SAID HE WOULD SURF OVER TO THE TREASURE MAP AND USE IT TO OPEN A PORTAL DOOR TO HIS HOME PLANET OF MONTRESSOR.

KAABOOOOMMM!!

HE GOT THE SHIP THROUGH JUST BEFORE TREASURE PLANET EXPLODED! AND UPON HIS RETURN TO THE SHIP, EVERYONE ON BOARD CHEERED AND THANKED HIM!

I'VE GOT A LITTLE JOB FOR YA, MORPHY. I NEED YA TO KEEP AN EYE ON THIS HERE PUP. WILL YA DO ME THAT FAVOR?

OH, AND HERE'S SOMETHING FOR YOUR DEAR MOTHER—TO REBUILD THAT INN O' HERS.

SILVER HAD SAVED SOME OF THE TREASURE AFTER ALL. AND HE GAVE IT TO JIM.

STAY OUT OF TROUBLE, YOU OLD SCALAWAG—OR I'LL COME FIND YOU.

JIMBO, WHEN HAVE I EVER DONE OTHERWISE?

HAVE FUN AT HOME . . . AND GOOD LUCK.

KAWHOOSH!

AND DO COME FIND ME SOMEDAY, LAD—I'LL BE THINKIN' OF YOU.

IN THE END, EVERYTHING TURNED OUT BEST FOR EVERYONE. CAPTAIN AMELIA AND DR. DOPPLER WERE MARRIED AND STARTED A FAMILY. AND THE CONSTABLES WERE BACK AT THE RECONSTRUCTED INN, BUT THIS TIME THEY WERE AWARDING JIM HIS CERTIFICATE FROM THE INTERSTELLAR ACADEMY!

JIM MAY HAVE LET FLINT'S TREASURE SLIP AWAY. BUT WHAT HE HAD LEARNED DURING HIS ADVENTURE—TO BELIEVE IN HIMSELF, TO CHART HIS COURSE AND STICK TO IT—WAS WORTH *MORE* THAN THE LOOT OF A THOUSAND WORLDS!

THE END